Maggie McGillicuddy's Eye for TROUBLE

For all my wonderful neighbors, past and present, young and old, next door, down the street and across the way — S.H.

To all the people who taught me that my imagination is a wonderful thing, especially my mom and dad — B.K.

Text © 2016 Susan Hughes
Illustrations © 2016 Brooke Kerrigan

Kids Can Press acknowledges the financial support of the Government of Ontario, through the Ontario Media Development Corporation's Ontario Book Initiative; the Ontario Arts Council; the Canada Council for the Arts; and the Government of Canada, through the CBF, for our publishing activity.

Published in Canada by
Kids Can Press Ltd.
25 Dockside Drive
Toronto, ON M5A 0B5

Published in the U.S. by
Kids Can Press Ltd.
2250 Military Road
Tonawanda, NY 14150

www.kidscanpress.com

The artwork in this book was rendered in watercolor, pencil crayon, gouache and collage. The text is set in Chronicle Text.

Edited by Stacey Roderick
Designed by Marie Bartholomew

This book is smyth sewn casebound.
Manufactured in Malaysia in 3/2016 by Tien Wah Press (Pte.) Ltd.

CM 16 0 9 8 7 6 5 4 3 2 1

Library and Archives Canada Cataloguing in Publication

Hughes, Susan, 1960–, author
    Maggie McGillicuddy's eye for trouble / written by
Susan Hughes ; illustrated by Brooke Kerrigan.

ISBN 978-1-77138-291-5 (hardback)

    I. Kerrigan, Brooke, illustrator II. Title.

PS8565.U42M33 2016   jC813'.54   C2015-907234-4

Kids Can Press is a **l'Orus**™ Entertainment company

Maggie
McGillicuddy's
Eye for
TROUBLE

Written by
Susan Hughes

Illustrated by
Brooke Kerrigan

Kids Can Press

Maggie McGillicuddy sat swinging and knitting on her porch, keeping an eye out for trouble.

(Trouble? Trouble here? Where all looked to be sleepy, snoring, ho-hum, boring? Well, you might not see it, but Maggie sure could. Oh, yes, there was plenty of trouble to be seen in this town, in this neighborhood, on this very street.)

It was Wednesday morning, and Maggie's new neighbors were moving in.

Out their front door came a stiff-legged dog slowly, slowly down the steps and tippy-toe, tippy-toe to the end of the walk. Then, *ka-powie*! A firecracker of a lad sprang from the steps and barreled down the walk.

"Wait for me, Cody Dog!" he cried.

Quickly his ma appeared, calling, "Come back, Charlie! You can't go out alone. What if you find trouble — or it finds you?"

Exactly! thought Maggie.

And a little later, Maggie did see it. Trouble!
A hungry tiger creeping, creeping across the lawn.
(You see it there, don't you? Charlie did, too.)

Maggie didn't hesitate.

Tickety, tickety, tack!

She clacked her knitting needles furiously,
scaring the stripes off that lily-livered wildcat.

Then, the next day, more trouble.

Bernie, the delivery girl, brought Maggie her Thursday afternoon pizza, just like always. But as Bernie jumped on her bike … a snake with a body as thick as an oak tree came slithering through the grass toward her!

(You see the snake, don't you? Well, that Bernie didn't! No imagination, I guess.)

Maggie didn't hesitate.

Whickety, whickety, whack!

She smacked her walking stick mightily, scaring the scales off that cowardly reptile.

On Friday, even more trouble.

Frank, the letter carrier, delivered Maggie's mail, just like always.

But as he was off to the next house ... a huge eagle with claws sharp as nails swooped toward him!

(You see the eagle, don't you? Well, that Frank didn't! No imagination, I guess.)

Maggie didn't hesitate.

Tickety, tickety, tack! Whickety, whickety, whack!

She clacked her knitting needles furiously
and smacked her walking stick mightily along
the rungs of the porch, scaring the feathers
off that yellow-bellied bird.

Now here it was Saturday, and Maggie McGillicuddy sat on her porch, swinging and knitting, just like always.

And out came stiff-legged Cody Dog, walking slowly, slowly down the steps and tippy-toe, tippy-toe to the end of the walk. Then, *ka-powie*! Charlie sprang from the steps and barreled past Cody Dog, right toward the road.

That Charlie was heading straight for trouble!

And there was nothing imaginary about *this* trouble. Maggie knew that for certain. A car was coming up the street!

Maggie catapulted out of her swing. Clacking her knitting needles and smacking her walking stick wouldn't solve *this* kind of trouble! Taking a deep breath, and with all the force she could muster, Maggie hollered:

You there, Charlie! Stop right now!

That road is trouble! That car is

TROUBLE!

Well, that did it. Maggie stopped Charlie right there in his tracks.

Maggie McGillicuddy slapped her hand to her chest and gasped with relief. Cody Dog gave his tail a little wag. And that real trouble went sailing on by.

With a big, wide grin, Charlie waved at Maggie and started whirling and bounding his way over to her. Old Cody Dog came, too, tippy-toeing, tippy-toeing.

But look!

"A herd of thirsty elephants, heading for a watering hole, running straight at me!" cried Charlie.

(You see those elephants, don't you? Of course you do, and Maggie did, too.)

Maggie was ready to clack her knitting needles, just in case. But Charlie flung his arms up in the air and roared, and Cody Dog wagged his tail defiantly. Those elephants took one look, flapped their big ears and thundered away, back across the savanna.

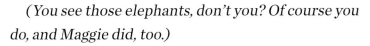

ROAR!

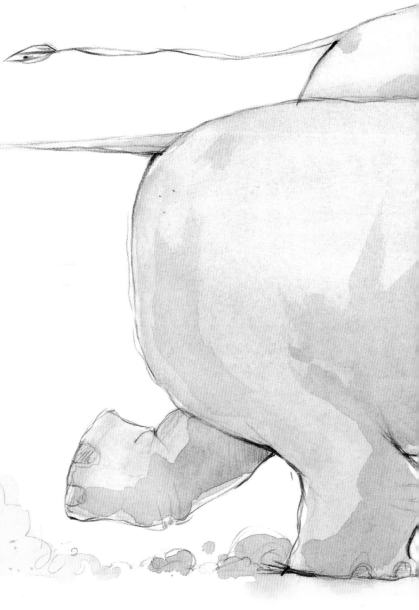

Then, more trouble.

"Watch out!" called Maggie. "A huge, hungry crocodile, jaws wide open, ready to chomp!"

(I know, I know. Charlie saw it. You see it. I'm not even going to ask!)

Maggie was ready to smack her walking stick, just in case. But Charlie showed off his karate skills, and Cody Dog chased his tail ferociously. That crocodile took one look, snapped its jaws shut and slipped away, back into the lagoon.

Finally, Charlie and Cody Dog reached the porch.

"Ma says I have a nose for some kinds of trouble," said Charlie. "But, Mrs. Maggie, you have an eye for *all* kinds of trouble!"

Maggie agreed.

She invited Charlie up on the porch with her, and the pair sat side by side, swinging. From there, they could see the most amazing kinds of trouble ever.

When Charlie got up to go, he asked, "Can Cody Dog and I come back tomorrow?"

Maggie thought that was a fine idea. And Charlie's ma did, too.

So now, almost every single morning, *ka-powie*! Charlie whirls and bounds his way over for a visit. And along goes Cody Dog, too, tippy-toeing, tippy-toeing.

Because Maggie McGillicuddy and her new friend Charlie know one thing is certain. There is plenty of trouble to be seen in this town, in this neighborhood, on this very street. You just have to keep an eye out for it!